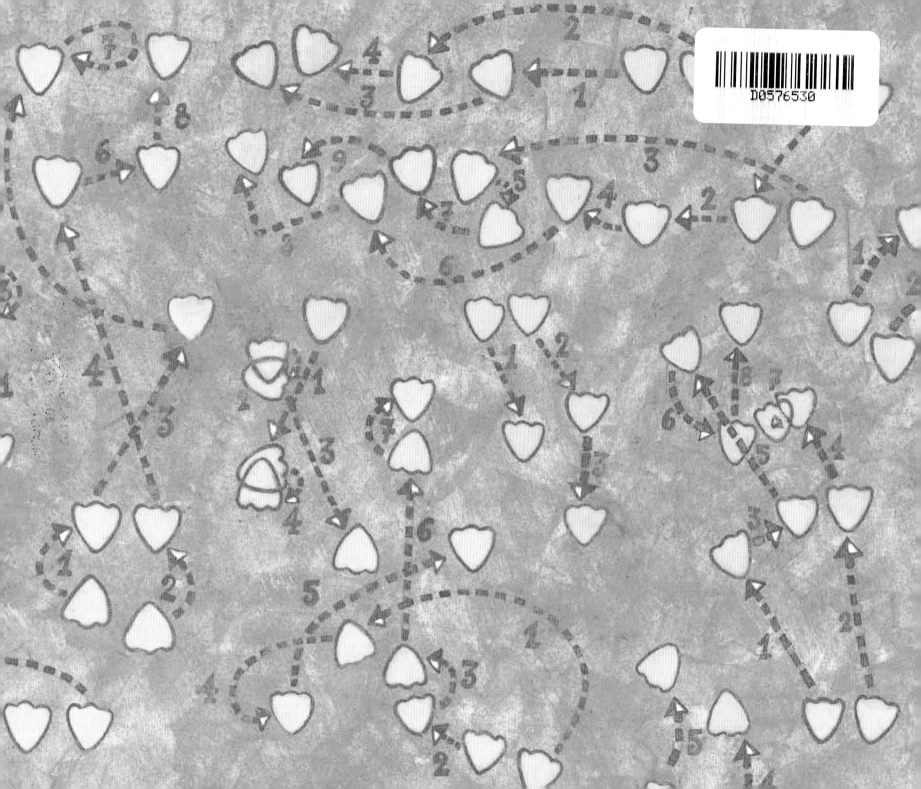

For Florence
and everyone who, at one time or another, has refused or will refuse to march in step.
— *J. F. D.*

THE GEESE MARCH IN STEP

Written and illustrated by
JEAN-FRANÇOIS DUMONT

Eerdmans Books for Young Readers

Grand Rapids, Michigan • Cambridge, U.K.

One day, as they did every day,
the geese on the farm lined up carefully to
go down to the pond for their morning swim.
Igor, the leader of the flock, started the
march by calling out the rhythm:
one, two; one, two; one, two.

Their webbed feet struck the ground perfectly in synch,
and their rumps waddled together in time. Igor was happy.
The other animals on the farm stopped to let the geese pass,
careful not to disrupt the parade.

On the farm, for as long as anyone could remember,
the geese had marched down to the pond in step.
No one knew exactly why — that's just the way it was.

Edgar the rat said they probably did it to work up some courage, given the temperature of the water. An old ram insisted that this was how the geese remembered the long trips they had taken to warm countries when they lived in the wild. But Igor just said, "Traditions are traditions!"and every morning he paraded along, proud of himself and his flock.

One, two; one, two; one, two . . . ^{tap}**; one, two . . .** ^{tap}

Igor pricked up his ears.

One, two . . . ^{tap}**; one, two . . .** ^{tap}

Igor frowned:

"Tap? What's that tap?"

Quacks of disapproval ran down the line.

One, two; one, two;
one, two . . . ^{tap}**; one, two . . .** ^{tap}
Finally, it was more than Igor could take!
With a single gesture, he ordered his flock to stop.

Igor tucked his wings behind his back. With a serious look on his face,
he worked his way down the column of geese standing motionless at attention,
until he reached a little goose who was blushing and staring at the ground.

"Are you the one who's disrupting the march, Zita?" Igor scolded.
"You've just arrived and you're already causing trouble!"

Zita wanted to speak up, to say that it wasn't her fault, that she wasn't used to marching in step, that it didn't really serve a purpose anyway, that she had been distracted by a cow who was grazing noisily in the field nearby, and that . . .

But Igor had no sympathy:
"Since you won't make any effort, I can't let you be in the parade.
You'll have to go down for your swim after we get there."

Seeing the entire flock giving her dirty looks, Zita didn't say a word. She just turned, head lowered, and walked back up the road to the farm. In the distance, she heard Igor calling out the rhythm for the flock
as it marched away:
One, two; *one, two;* one, two . . .

A few minutes later, Zita headed back down the road toward the pond. "I'm really no good as a goose," she thought. "It's not that hard, anyway, to march in step. You just have to do what everyone else is doing:

One, two; one, two; one, two!
Even Annabelle can do it, and she's as thick as her two webbed feet!"

"One, two; one, two!"

Zita's eyes filled with tears.

"One, two; one, two.

Why am I not like the other geese?

One, two; one, two.

They're always so obedient and so focused!"

Zita passed two piglets from the Rose and Brown families.
They were also going down for a swim. "Hey, you, new little
goose! Why aren't you with the others?" Bruno called out.

"Hey, you, new little goose! What are you sniffling about, and
why are you dragging your feet like that?" Rosalie asked.

But Zita didn't see them. She just kept crying.
"It's really not even all that complicated. Why can't I do it?"

Splash, splash and splash again ^{sniff} splash

went her little webbed feet on the wet ground.

"I can't even walk normally," Zita sniffled.

Splash sniff splash and splash again sniff splash

Splash sniff splash and sniff splash again sniff splash

"Hey, that's kind of a nice tune," a woodpecker thought, busy hammering at a tree. And without even realizing it, he joined in Zita's tune with his beak:

Splash sniff splash knock and sniff splash again knock sniff splash knock

Splash sniff splash knock and sniff splash again knock sniff splash knock

Raymond the rooster was pecking in the ditch when he heard Zita.
"Wow, that music makes you want to shake your tail feathers!"
And without realizing it, still pecking the ground in search of a worm,
he joined in with the little goose, too.

peck peck peck *peck peck peck* *peck* *peck peck peck* *peck peck peckity peck*

Splash sniff splash knock and sniff splash again knock sniff splash knock

peck peck peck *peck peck peck* *peck* *peck peck peck* *peck peck peckity peck*

Splash sniff splash knock and sniff splash again knock sniff splash knock

"That little goose really knows how to make animals move!" the donkey and the cow thought as they watched the parade go by. And without realizing it, they joined in with Zita, too.

peck peck peck   peck peck peck   peck   peck peck peck   peck peck peckity peck

Splash sniff splash knock and sniff splash again knock sniff splash knock

Heeeee hawwww   **Moooooooooooo**

"That beat's enough to uncurl a sheep's wool!"
said Denise the sheep, grazing in the field nearby.
"If I didn't have hooves, I think I would snap my fingers!"

peck peck peck   *peck peck peck*   *peck*   *peck peck peck*   *peck peck peckity peck*

Splash sniff splash knock and sniff splash again knock sniff splash knock

Heeeee hawwww   Mooooooooooo

Baaaaaa baaaaaa   baaaaaa baaaaaa   baaaaaa baaaaaa

By the time the little goose reached the pond, much to Igor's shock, Zita was at the head of the most unbelievable parade ever seen. From the gobbling turkey to the bleating sheep, from the whinnying horse to the croaking frog, all of the animals were joined in a wild rhythm that swept along everything in its path.

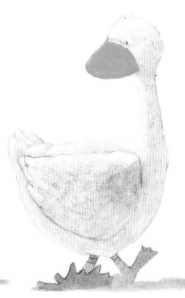

After that day, there was no more marching in step. Igor kept up his **"One, two; one, two!"** all by himself, but no one followed him. The whole farm was waiting eagerly for Zita to head down to the pond . . .

© Éditions Flammarion, 2007
87, quai Panhard et Levassor – 75647 Paris Cedex 13
www.editions.flammarion.com
Originally published in French under the title
La petite oie qui ne voulait pas marcher au pas
by Éditions Flammarion, 2007
This English language translation © Eerdmans Books for Young Readers

Published in 2014 by Eerdmans Books for Young Readers,
an imprint of Wm. B. Eerdmans Publishing Co.
2140 Oak Industrial Dr. NE
Grand Rapids, Michigan 49505
P.O. Box 163, Cambridge CB3 9PU U.K.

www.eerdmans.com/youngreaders

Manufactured at Tien Wah Press
in Malaysia in October 2013, first printing

19 18 17 16 15 14   9 8 7 6 5 4 3 2 1

Library of Congress Cataloging-in-Publication Data

Dumont, Jean-François, 1959- author, illustrator.
The geese march in step / by Jean-François Dumont ;
illustrated by Jean-François Dumont.
pages cm
Summary: "Zita just can't seem to march to the same beat as the
rest of the geese, but before long, she realizes, as do the other
barnyard animals, that her own special rhythm is just right."
— Provided by publisher.
ISBN 978-0-8028-5443-8
[1. Individuality — Fiction. 2. Rhythm — Fiction. 3. Geese — Fiction.
4. Domestic animals — Fiction.] I. Title.
PZ7.D89367Ge 2014
[E] — dc23
2013031003

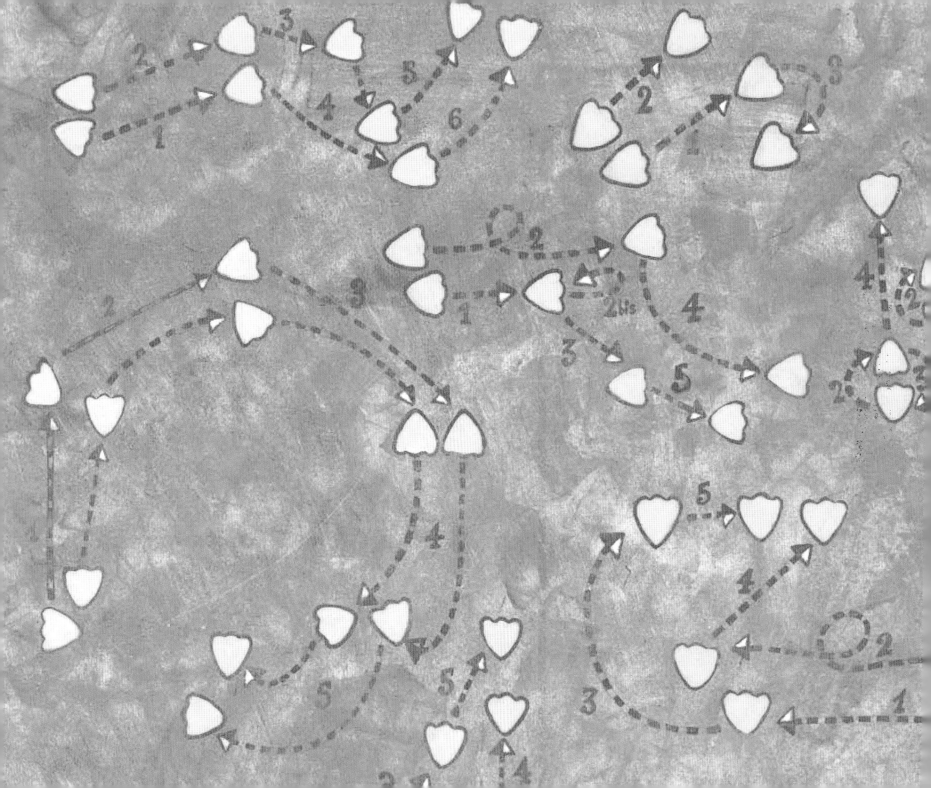